THE
Iciest, Diciest, Scariest
Sled Ride Ever!

by Rebecca Rule

Illustrated by Jennifer Thermes

The LaPierre Brothers

Published by Islandport Press
P.O. Box 10
267 U.S. Route One, Suite B
Yarmouth, Maine 04096
books@islandportpress.com
www.islandportpress.com

Job / Batch#: 108739   Production Date: June, 2012

Plant & Location: Printed by Everbest Printing Co. Ltd., Guangdong, China

ISBN: 978-1-934031-88-9
Library of Congress Control Number: 2012934445

Patty P. and Patty H.

Islandport Press, P.O. Box 10, Yarmouth, Maine 04096
books@islandportpress.com
www.islandportpress.com

ISLANDPORT PRESS   YARMOUTH • MAINE

Me! (Lizzie)   Robert   Chipper!

For my mother and for my father, Lewis W. "Bud" Barker,
also known as Grampa Bud
—REBECCA RULE

For Petey and Robbie, my two little brothers
—JENNIFER THERMES

THE
Iciest, Diciest, Scariest
Sled Ride Ever!

by Rebecca Rule

Illustrated by Jennifer Thermes

On the first day of February vacation, sleet
followed snow and made a crust so thick you
couldn't break through even if you jumped
on it as hard as you could.

The largest of the three LaPierre brothers tried. He jumped up and down, but he couldn't break through.

My little brother, Robert, slid down the slope in our back yard like a hockey puck in the puffy snowsuit he got for Christmas. He bumped into the snow-softened stone wall.

It looked like fun, so we all tried it — the LaPierres, my two best friends, Patty H. and Patty P., and me. We bounced off the stone wall, then had to form a human chain to pull everybody back up the little hill.

The world was ice and we were skaters without skates.

We decided to look for a really good sliding place.

Patty H. tested her snow saucer on the hill by
Raymond's Brook. She spun all
the way down—"aahhhhhhhh!"—
plowing backwards through the puckerbrush
at the bottom. I got ready to go.

"Forget it, Lizzie," she yelled up to me.

"You can't steer on this stuff."

"We'll meet you at the bridge," I yelled down.

Then I remembered the old travis sled in Grampa Bud's barn.
It was homemade: two double-runner sleds hitched to
a plank seat.

When Grampa Bud was a kid, he said you could push off from his house at the stroke of noon, whiz down Old Mountain Road past the horse farm, past the mill, and past the blacksmith shop, whip around the curve, go past the cemetery, past the church, and past the skating pond, swoosh into the village, and spin to a stop in the snowbank by the gazebo before the bell finished ringing the hour.

"Course, then it took us the rest of the afternoon to hike home," Grampa Bud said.

"Please," we said. "Please, please."

"I don't know about this," he said. "It's awful icy." We promised not to break the travis.

"Just don't hurt yourselves," he said. "Hit a soft spot in the crust, things could get dicey." We promised not to break ourselves.

"It's hard to steer on crust," Grampa Bud said. "You get going too fast, it's pretty scary." "We're not scared," we said. "We'll try to go slow."

We were pretty sure he didn't believe us about the slow part. We didn't believe ourselves.

"And stay out of the road," he warned. "Times have changed."

An icy glaze coated the highest, mightiest, iciest sledding hill off Old Mountain Road. We'd sledded here before—on saucers, cardboard boxes, and once on my cousin Poppie's Flexible Flyer—but never on a sled as big as Grampa Bud's travis. And never on crust like this.

The smooth surface was so bright, it hurt our eyes. The hill top glared in the sun.

Two LaPierre boys pulled the travis. Patty P. pushed.

We couldn't stand once it got steep. Our legs kept slipping right out from under us.

So we crawled.

I could hear Robert's snowsuit swishing behind me.
He grabbed my boot. I tried to shake him loose.

We both rolled all the way down the hill and wedged
up against a small hemlock tree.

Soon the three LaPierres, the two Pattys,
and the travis joined us.

"We need climbing ropes and pitons," the LaPierres said.

"We need cleats," Patty P. said.

"We'll never make it," Patty H. said.

"We need sticky mittens," Robert said, "and spiky knees."

"We need a hot air balloon," I said,
"for floating up."

We locked hands and feet. Then, on our bellies, we wormed up the slope—an inchworm train with a travis caboose.

We made it almost halfway before a LaPierre lost his grip.

"I'm going," he cried, and went—taking a Patty or two with him.

I rolled over, threw up my hands and
enjoyed the ride—all the way down.

Pig Pile!

"Let's go to my house and have cocoa,"
Patty H. said.

But we ignored her.

We took to the trees at the edge of the field. A LaPierre
tied the travis to his waist with the sled's pulling rope.
The crust seemed softer here, soft enough to dig in a toe.

We hugged trees all the slip-slide way to the top.
The three LaPierre boys formed a human chain
with the travis at the end of it.

Once we reached the height of land, we followed
the ridge to the top of the highest, mightiest, iciest
sledding hill off Old Mountain Road.

We saw white, bright mountains.

We saw the racing horse weathervane
on the roof of Grampa Bud's barn.

We saw the steeple of the church.

We saw the frozen pond.

No one said, "I am afraid." But we were, a little.

We played "one potato, two potato" to see who would steer. I won.

Behind me, my brother, the two Pattys,
and the three LaPierres squished together.

Ready?

Set?

The highest, mightiest, iciest sledding hill off
Old Mountain Road stretched before us like
a lifetime. I straightened the steer bar and
braced my knees. Robert buried his runny
nose in my back. The last LaPierre gave a
little push.

Off we went!

Slow at first—then fast—then faster.

Someone screamed.

It was me.

The runners on the old travis remembered how to glide.

The hill took control, and we were
flying, flying, over the highest,
mightiest, iciest sledding hill off
Old Mountain Road.

We were going so fast the tears blew out of our eyes.

We were going so fast we forgot to be scared.

Some of us laughed.

Some of us screamed.

Some of us did both at the same time.

The wind whipped our screams and laughter like a beautiful scarf trailing wildly behind.

At the bottom, Robert crawled out from under the pile of LaPierres, Pattys, and me —with the travis bottoms-up on top.

He wiped his nose with his mitten.

He gazed in wonder up that long steep slope we'd just careened down.

He said, "Let's do it again."

So we did.

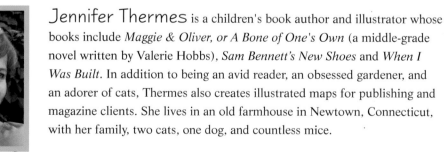

Travis sleds (that's what we called them in my family) are long runner sleds that could carry anywhere from two to twelve to 100 people. They were much more common in the early- and mid- twentieth century than they are now. They are believed to have descended from the travois, a Native American style of sled, usually made with two joined crossed poles, that was pulled by dogs or horses. The travoy, a similar type of sled, was used in the logging industry to haul lumber. Someone along the way realized runners would make these summertime sleds useful—and more fun—in winter.

The Uncle Sam Sled, considered the world's longest sled, was a travis sled built in the 1890s in Farmington, New Hampshire, by Hervey Pearl. At seventy-seven feet long, it could seat at least seventy adults or 100 children. Mr. Pearl's fast and furious runs down Main Street grew quite famous until, with the rise of the motor car, Uncle Sam was retired in 1922. It is now on display at the New Hampshire Farm Museum in Milton, N.H.

Rebecca Rule is the author of *Live Free and Eat Pie!* and *Headin' for the Rhubarb: A New Hampshire Dictionary (well, kinda)*. She is also the author of three short story collections about New Hampshire, including *The Best Revenge*, named Outstanding Work of Fiction by the New Hampshire Writer's Project. Rule is best known for her live storytelling events, many sponsored by the New Hampshire Humanities Council. She chronicles many of these events, and her encounters with people and language, in her blog, "Travels with Becky," which can be found at www. livefreeandeatpie.com. A graduate of the University of New Hampshire, she taught writing classes there for a number of years. She has lived in New Hampshire all her life (so far). She lives in Northwood with her husband, John Rule, their wire fox terrier, Bob, and various other dogs, cats, and birds.

Jennifer Thermes is a children's book author and illustrator whose books include *Maggie & Oliver, or A Bone of One's Own* (a middle-grade novel written by Valerie Hobbs), *Sam Bennett's New Shoes* and *When I Was Built*. In addition to being an avid reader, an obsessed gardener, and an adorer of cats, Thermes also creates illustrated maps for publishing and magazine clients. She lives in an old farmhouse in Newtown, Connecticut, with her family, two cats, one dog, and countless mice.